MY DOG IS SO BIG

Flori, you're the best!
Good Luck Always
Maggie G.
2017

RoseDog Books
585 Alpha Drive
Suite 103
Pittsburgh, PA 15238
Visit our website at www.rosedogbookstore.com

ISBN: 978-1-4809-6720-5
eISBN: 978-1-4809-6743-4

MY DOG IS SO BIG

by Maggie Greene

illustrations by Betty Graves

RoseDog Books

PITTSBURGH, PENNSYLVANIA 15238

MY DOG IS SO SO BIG

HE'S AS TALL AS MOM

MY DOG IS SO BIG

I NEED A TRUCK

FOR HIM TO SIT IN

MY DOG LIKES HORSES... ... ...

... ...AND

...   .CATS, AND ...   .

LITTLE KIDS

MY DOG HATES BATHS

BUT, HE LIKES THE SNOW AND...

PEOPLE'S LAPS

MY DOG LIKES TO SLEEP ALOT

AND ON HIS BACK, SOMETIMES

MY DOG LIKES TO PLAY WITH OTHER DOGS

MY DOG LIKES TO SMELL THE FLOWERS ALONG THE WAY

MY DOG WASN'T ALWAYS SO BIG

MY DOG SMILES A LOT, AND ... ...

MY DOG HAS

LOTS OF FRIENDS

THIS FRIEND FORGOT TO LOOK

WHEN HE CROSSED THE STREET

MY DOG IS
BIG AND
WONDERFUL

WOULDN'T YOU LIKE
A BIG DOG
LIKE HIM?

THE END